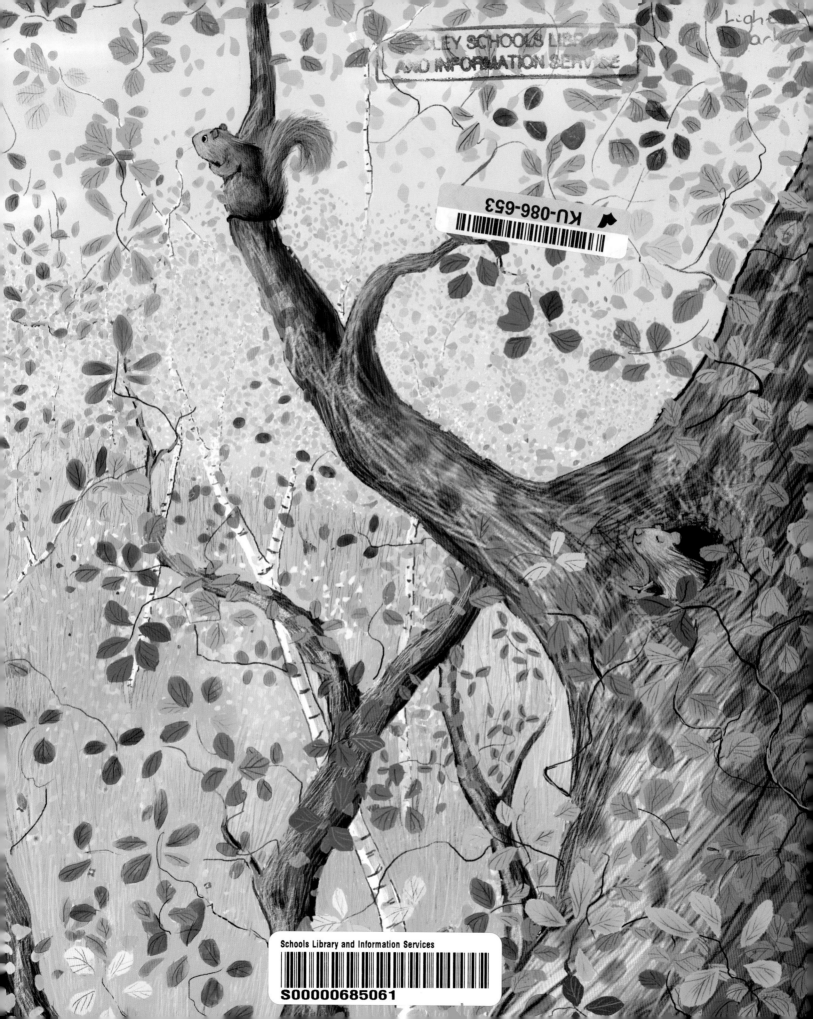

To my sister, Adria

Copyright © Jessica Meserve, 2006
The rights of Jessica Meserve to be identified as the author and illustrator of this work
have been asserted by her in accordance with the Copyright, Designs and Patents Act, 1988.
First published in Great Britain in 2006 by Andersen Press Ltd, 20 Vauxhall Bridge Road,
London SW1V 2SA. Published in Australia by Random House Australia Pty.,
20 Alfred Street, Milsons Point, Sydney, NSW 2061. All rights reserved.
Colour separated in Switzerland by Photolitho AG, Zürich.
Printed and bound in Italy by Grafiche AZ, Verona.

10   9   8   7   6   5   4   3   2   1

British Library Cataloguing in Publication Data available.

ISBN-10: 1 84270 517 2
ISBN-13: 978 1 84270 517 9
This book has been printed on acid-free paper

Small

Jessica Meserve

Andersen Press • London

Small had a **problem.**
She was stuck in Big's shadow.

Small tried to jump higher,
but Big was bouncier.

Small tried to escape,
but Big was faster.

And Big always got
the best presents.

Sometimes Big tried
to scare Small.

One day Big made
Small very angry,

so Small did something very mean.

Big's parrot flew away.

When Big
found out . . .

. . . Small felt
even smaller.

The next day,
Small decided
to leave.

Nobody noticed.

Small
was free.

She tried to feel happy,

but she
was too
lonely.

High in the tree,
Small saw Big's parrot.

Low on the ground,
Small saw . . .

. . . Big.
Big was too
scared to climb
the tree.

Small
wasn't
scared.

Small felt BRAVE.

Small felt **BIG**.

Small felt very happy.

And best of all,
Small was no longer
stuck in Big's shadow.